Camellia Manor

Cindy Webb Morris

Camellia Manor

Radical Bookshop and Press
4838 Richard Road SW, Suite 300
Calgary, AB T3E 6L1

Copyright 2024 by Cindy Webb Morris

FIC029000 - Fiction, Short Stories

All rights reserved. No part of this publication may be reproduced, stored in a retrieval system or transmited in any form or by any means, electronic, mechanical, photocopying, recording or otherwise without the prior permision of the author.

June 1, 2024

Editor: Charlotte Hayes-Clemens
Cover Design: Lexie Angelo

Typeset in IvyOra

ISBN-13: 978-1-990201-18-9

Printed in the United States

*To my late husband, Warren,
who never read a book in his life, but loved
me and supported my writing.*

contents

CHAPBOOK

Camellia Manor 9

Acknowledgements

About the Author

Camellia Manor

"I need something special," I say to my husband, "something that cleanses my spirit, ignites my imagination, and completes my spiritual journey."

I've almost convinced Jack to take me to my favourite shop to buy my anniversary gift. But he hesitates on the threshold. "This place is creepy," he says. "A witch lives here."

"Don't be ridiculous." I pull on his sleeve.

"I'm not kidding. My buddies at the Whiskey Holler told me she curses any men that go in her shop."

I shake my head. "They're just plain stupid," I tell him. "Dumb, dumb, dumb."

I've been trying to get Jack into the Queen Moonfall Curio Shop for ages and I'm not going to be stopped by the nonsense spouted by some local yokels.

"Ok, ok. Stop pulling on me. I'll go in."

A sweet tinkle from the bell hanging over the door welcomes us in. Jack follows me around until he comes across some fountain pens for his collection, while I carry on to the back of the shop. I feel a warm wave of pleasure ensnare me and draw me to a watercolour image on the wall. I am enchanted. It is a portrait of a house. An echo of recognition resounds. I know this house, I want this house, I will have this house.

"You found me," the image whispers from its antique frame. "You found me. Take me home." I gently release it from its hook and carry it to the front of the store.

"A painting of a Victorian house?" Jack grunts. "Really, Louise, you want a ten-dollar picture for your present?"

"Yes," I say. "It speaks to me. It's beckoning me to buy it." I ignore his laughter: I'm used to his derisive attitude.

Jack pulls out his wallet and hands over a twenty to Sabrina Morgan, the proprietor. Sabrina is one of my favourite people in the neighbourhood. A treasured odd duck, with waist-long grey hair topped by a Celtic tiara, shimmering purple eyeshadow, and thin gold bangles jingling from her wrists to her elbows. No one will ever accuse her of being boring. People accuse her of other things, muttering under their breath and crossing themselves when they pass by her shop. Her black cat, Ewart, and the bowl of crystals by the cash register add to her eccentricity. I like Sabrina's quirkiness. She understands me in ways my husband struggles to grasp. I'm happy I was able to direct my husband into my friend's unique shop, despite his efforts to steer me away.

Sabrina thanks Jack as she hands back his change. She leans over the counter and winks at me. "It's an extraordinary picture," she says. "Let your imagination guide you through the doorway. A myriad of adventures await you. But, heed this warning. A time will come when the doors and windows of the manor are slammed shut forever."

I ponder her odd comment for a moment then simply smile and

say goodbye. Jack snorts and rolls his eyes at the pair of us as we leave the store.

On the drive home I admire my gift. The two-storey Victorian resembles a Hansel and Gretel gingerbread house. Painted bubble-gum pink like my favourite candy, with scalloped licorice-black iron edges tucked beneath eaves from which hang two earthen baskets filled with red-candy-apple camellias. The same flowers bloom from two butterscotch-coloured pots flanking the marshmallow-white door. My mouth waters. I love sweet things.

It is the house of my dreams.

My husband doesn't understand the significance of this house, or of its deep meaning to me.

Now, three years later, I am sitting down at my desk and gazing at the watercolour image. When the clock chimes midnight, I close my eyes. An encouraging warmth invades my body. A sign that it's time for me to enter. The silence I encounter is comforting. I need no one to escort me past the pink camellia shrubs lining the walkway and take me up the toffee-toned wooden steps to the front door. I've been here many times before.

I turn the giant Scotch mint doorknob and step inside. A familiar scent greets me. I stand still and breathe in the fresh minty smell of peppermint patties, the spicy odour of crystallized ginger, the sensual aroma of vanilla fudge, and the toasted nutty bouquet of dark chocolate. This is my candy shop. My safe haven. It exists for me and me alone.

I walk around the kitchen, living room, and bedroom. Everywhere, there are wooden barrels filled to the brim with hard candy: barley toys, Macintosh toffee, and peppermint sticks. On oak tables and shelves sit blue and white porcelain bowls overflowing with other confectionary delights. Chicken bones: spicy, hard shells with creamy, unsweetened chocolate filling. Chewy caramel bites. Crunchy peanut clusters. Succulent strawberry champagne truffles. Juicy fruit jellies. The gift-wrapped boxes of Pal-O-Mine bars tempt me, a delicious combination of fudge and peanuts enrobed in chocolate. It is a difficult decision but I pop my chosen treat into my mouth and savour its deliciousness. A sigh of satisfaction escapes my lips.

"Where did you get that?"

The deep voice startles me, and I exit my dream house. I turn. My son is standing before me, eyebrows raised and pointing a finger at the Pal-0-Mine wrappers in my hand.

"You know you're not supposed to be eating candy, Mom."

I savour the last bit of chocolate before speaking. "I know, Simon, I know."

"If Dad was here, he'd be upset that you're not taking care of yourself."

"It was just this once, Son."

He shakes his head and goes down to the basement where he'll spend the day sorting out his father's belongings—something I've been reluctant to tackle. I'm grateful for his assistance.

When he is safely out of sight, I focus again on my candy haven and notice I've left the front door ajar. I'll go back and close it after Simon's gone home. For now, it will remain open until I sneak back in to dive into the barrel of chocolate cherries I spied earlier.

My door is shut, my windows shuttered, my ashes scattered to the wind. I exist only in a portrait, lovingly crafted by a young man who once dwelled within my walls. A budding artist, he painted my likeness before disaster destroyed me, his talent saving my life.

I was built in the town of Woodstock. The designer and builder—
Sir Christopher Wren's less-known third cousin, twice-removed,
Palmerston Wren—used strong Scottish pine from the Highlands
for the frame and the finest mahogany for most of the interior. A
magnificent winding staircase to the second floor, polished oak floors
throughout, and a steep gabled roof were just a few of my stunning
features.

From the top of a hill, I surveyed the bustling townsfolk as they
shopped from farmers who'd driven in from the country with their
harvests. Thoroughbreds were tied to iron railings along the street
and draft horses pulled wagons loaded with goods. Children darted
through the crowds. I felt truly lucky to be in this spot. It was from
this viewpoint, I realized that I was deaf to the outside world. I could
see mouths opening and shutting but heard only the chatters coming
from the men working inside my walls.

A year dragged on as I waited for my owners to arrive from Ireland.
I was lonely. My walls ached with intense longing. Finally, when an
older gentleman came to show a young couple around my rooms, I
learned the Barrett family had perished on the sea voyage to Canada
and I was left to a distant relative from England.

I was overjoyed when Charles and Lucy Webb moved in and
started decorating. The pretty pink Lucy chose for my exterior, in
spite of her husband's protest, thrilled me. She took such pleasure
in the sweetly scented pink camellia shrubs she planted along the
walkway and the bright red petunias she hung from the eaves and
placed in pots by the front door. And in turn, they gave me a deep
pride.

I'd been by myself so long that I hungered for their conversations
and for the joy they brought into my life. One of those joys was
the birth of their son, Perry. I loved the little boy as if he was my
own. I celebrated his birthdays and enjoyed hearing his laughter
reverberating through my rooms. I was the first to recognize his

artistic leanings, but never imagined they would someday be used to save me.

The picture of a Victorian house, a twenty-fifth wedding anniversary gift from my husband, is painted Valentine's pink like his favourite Victoria's Secret negligee. Nightly, as I admire my treasured artwork, my body floods with a warmth that stirs my desire to erase all distance between my lover's world and mine. I drink in the passionate red camellias that cascade down from the corners of the house. Their earthen baskets hang from the solid heart-shaped iron trim under the eaves. Pots of matching flowers flank the virgin-white front door. My true love—my beloved, who never understood my devotion to this place—awaits my return.

It is the house of my dreams.

As I nestle in my hot-pink recliner, the clock strikes twelve. It's time for me to enter. I close my eyes. A frenzy of heat ignites my body. I need no one to guide me down the red-camellia-lined walkway, nor assist me up the solid wooden steps to the front door. It's a familiar journey. I turn the smooth ivory doorknob and step inside. My breath quickens. My heart beats a wanton tattoo of pulsating passion that threatens to bring me to the floor. The sensual aroma of woodsy cologne greets me. This is my heaven, my paradise.

I stride quickly past the living room, and the royal-blue brocade sofa where we last made love. Tonight, I'm headed for the bedroom. Impatient with longing, every inch of my skin craves to be touched, to be fondled, to be loved. I shove open the door with a force that betrays my excitement.

14

"Well, well," drawls a husky voice. "Someone's in a hurry."

I fling myself through gauzy white curtains and dive onto the sumptuous four-poster bed. Jack grins as he grabs me and sits me atop his waist. His coal-black hair hangs down past his shoulders. His blue eyes weaken me. His strong, firm chest beckons me. We join together in holy matrimonial pleasure. My skin flushes and I thrust out my bosom in an unmistakable invitation. I lean forward with my offering and whisper, "You are the greatest gift." What follows is something I cannot describe with mere words.

I am back in my lounger, grinning from ear to ear, when a deep voice interrupts my pleasure.

"Mother, what the hell are you smiling about?"

I turn and stare at my son.

Simon shakes his head. "Why are you still in your pyjamas? It's two o'clock. If you want me to help you move that stuff out of the basement, you better get dressed quick. I don't have all day you know."

"I know, Son, I know. I'll get dressed."

He closes his eyes and takes a deep breath. "I'll be down in the basement."

As soon as he is out of sight, I take a last peek at my love nest and notice I've left the front door ajar. I'll go back and close it after my son is gone. For now, it will stay open until I can safely return and indulge in the erotic pleasures within its walls.

One of the first additions Charles Webb made within my walls was to bring in the latest technology: electric light. I overheard the installers telling him he was the first one on the block to invest in this new invention and they expected many would soon emulate him. The light warmed me. I was proud but Charles was even prouder. His chest swelled at their comment. He bought several new inventions that first year. A Bell telephone, a Baldwin Refrigerator icebox, a Kodak camera, and a Remington typewriter, which he used to write his memoir. The brand names of those products are seared into my memory as Charles boasted, over and over, to anyone who entered his domain. Lucy, however, was not given the newest method of cleaning floors and carpets: the Bissell vacuum, as her husband believed the scrub brushes and rug beaters kept her busy and fit.

In spite of his thirst for consequence in his neighbourhood, Charles abhorred having strangers in his home and would only allow gardeners to keep up a prosperous front, tending the camellias along the entry path. He did invite several business acquaintances to join him at Camellia Manor for drinks in his study. His wife stayed quiet in the background. Sadly, no one paid calls on Lucy once they realized she wouldn't open the door to their knocks. Their only glimpse of my lady would have been at the opera on the rare occasions her husband took her out of the house. It seemed to me that Charles was missing the best opportunities to improve his status. But then, I'm just a house, and I only heard what went on within my walls. I did enjoy the times Lucy got dressed up for an evening out. Her floor-length satin gowns were a startling contrast to her everyday cotton shift. The peacock-blue cape she always wore on top matched her unusual eye colour. A hidden fairy princess let out of her box for a brief moment.

As strange and disturbing as Charles' treatment was of his wife, he was a loving father who took a strong and kindly interest in his son. Perry was his pride and joy. Charles didn't allow Perry to have a governess, nor did he allow him to attend a boarding school. Instead, he taught Perry himself. Every night, when Charles came home from his banking position at Hoare & Co., he would sit his son down and grill him on what he'd studied during the day.

One time, I heard the pair discussing an article from the *Gazette*. Perry laughed so hard he fell off his chair. It was something about a bull escaping and charging through a sweetshop window in the town square. The same sweetshop his father had taken him to on an outing the week before.

"I hope the bull didn't ruin all the lollies," Perry laughed.

"Oh, I'm sure there will be plenty of lollies and sugarplums and bonbons for you next time we go," said Charles.

On another outing, the two travelled by steam train to the seaside, and I enjoyed hearing about it when Perry related his adventures to his mother later that evening.

"Oh, Mummy, you should have seen me. I waded out in the water up to my waist. It was so cold. And then I fell in and got wet all over including my hair. It was so much fun."

"It sounds like it, darling. And I saw from your clothes you played in the sand." Lucy smiled at her son, then glared at her husband. Charles simply shrugged and nodded toward Perry.

"I built a sandcastle and Dad helped me and it was the biggest sandcastle on the beach."

"Of course it was. Your father wouldn't want anything less than the biggest."

Charles walked out the door, oblivious to her sarcasm.

"Hop into bed, my darling boy, and I'll read you some more adventures of Alice in Wonderland." Lucy tucked her son in and stroked his forehead. She read the next chapter of Alice's adventure while he listened intently. When she finished, she kissed his forehead.

As she was leaving the room, Perry yawned and said, "Mummy, I wish you had come with us."

She choked up. "Me too, darling, me too."

When she went downstairs, her husband was pulling on his coat.

"I'm going to my club," he said, "don't wait up for me."

Lucy nodded and shut the door behind him. She sighed deeply as she leaned against it.

I'd noticed that Charles had been spending more and more time away from home. He told his wife he was going to his club, but I was suspicious. There's no hiding the odour of cheap perfume.

It's nearing the witching hour. I stand in front of my fridge, staring at the watercolour held in a magnetic frame. Blood from the slab of fresh meat I slammed on the cutting board seeps onto the counter and drips to the floor. Its red juices have splashed across the walkway in the picture. As I pull the cleaver out of the knife block, my focus remains on the Victorian house painted flesh pink. Blood-red camellias sit in iron pots on either side of the front entrance and in earthen baskets hanging from the eaves. The dirt-brown steps remind me of my husband's grave. I haven't visited Jack in months. The ghost-white doors warn me of the demons within the walls. They shadow my soul. They echo my shame.

The spectral work of art was an anniversary gift from my husband, which I later realized was his attempt at atonement. He could never have known how much this house would mirror my desires and give me the power to purify my soul. When the clock chimes the twelfth note, a fiery spear pierces my chest and yanks me into the image, where I find myself standing at the front door of the house. I blink several times and plead with myself to flee but I know in my heart that I will not listen. I never listen. With a sigh, I grip the bone handle and open the door. Why did I come here again?

It is the house of my nightmares.

When I step inside, the icy foyer chills me. I shiver and hesitate for a second, but an unseen force propels me forward. *Fears have to be faced,* my therapist told me, but I'm sure she never faced a fear like this one. Near the kitchen, a coppery odour invades my nostrils. I recognize it but keep going. I pass the cauldron of blood in the hallway. It was half full on my last visit. Now it overflows onto the wooden floor. The sticky substance marks my footprints to the living room. A skeleton chair with a skull headrest sits next to a small table. I look closer.. It's new since my last visit. Human femurs hold up the table. A leg is a leg, after all. The tabletop sends a frisson of excitement up my spine. Leathered skin stretched and nailed to a wooden board; a tanned pelt with a tattoo of the Tasmanian devil clearly showing. I laugh. So this is where my husband's lover disappeared to. I spit on the tattoo as I recall the last time I saw it.

I confronted the cow, the day after Jack confessed his sins. *You should never have provoked the bitch in me,* I told her. *He's mine, all mine. I'll kill you for taking him away from me.* She had the nerve to laugh when I showed her my pistol. I had the nerve to fire it. *Goodbye unbeliever,* I shouted as I pulled the trigger. I guess I really showed her.

I dredge up more spit and watch it drip slowly onto the tabletop.

A ribbon of white satin, like the lining of a coffin, appears in the air before me and I follow as it drifts out of the living room and up the stairs to the bedroom. It pushes the door open. I am confronted with the smell of rotting flesh. The stench nearly knocks me over. I hesitate to enter but a hard knock on the back of my head warns me not to wait. I hold my breath and step inside. A decaying body lies on top of the bed. The skin is marbled and some of it has slithered onto the floor. A legion of blowflies crawls out of a gaping hole in its middle and buzzes around my head. I swat them away.

He is no longer the man I once loved.

"Let's see how she likes you now, hotshot," I sneer.

I jump back into my kitchen when I hear my son's voice.

"Simon, you scared the bejesus out of me."

His look is puzzled and judgemental at the same time. "What time did you say they'd be here?"

"Who?"

Simon laughs. "Oh Mum, you've always got your head in a cloud. The trash guys are coming to clear out the basement."

I nod. "Yes, yes, of course."

"Hey, you should have an apron on. You've got blood and some other shit running down your shirt. And it stinks."

"I'll put the meat back in the fridge and change into a clean shirt."

"Sure thing. I'll go downstairs and check things out before they get here." He clatters down the stairs and out of sight.

I set the bowl of meat back in the fridge. As I close the fridge, I notice the door to the house in the picture has been left ajar. I cross myself and promise not to go back but I know, without a doubt, that I will return to the scene of my crime.

I couldn't have envisioned what would happen when I waved goodbye to Lucy as she set off to visit Perry at his college. I was accustomed to a home of civilized conversation and restrained shows of affection. There were elements of trouble lurking under the surface, but nothing like the malevolence that entered the house that day.

Charles' mistress was bold, with fiery hair that matched her brassy behaviour. I tried my best to shoo the wanton woman out of the house by opening all the windows and re-opening the front door she'd slammed shut. But she managed to escape my efforts and run straight into Charles' arms. He swooped her up and carried her to the marital bed.

Oh shame, I thought. *How could you?* I creaked and quaked as best I could but he would not be stopped. I was about to use my energy to tip over the dresser when I heard footsteps racing up the stairs and then a breathless voice. I tried to warn Lucy by rattling the light fixtures but she ignored me. When she pushed open the bedroom door, I shuddered.

"Charlie, I forgot Perry's cricket breeches—"

The bedclothes were scattered across the room. The hussy was on her knees. Charles was moaning. He stared at his wife.

There was dead silence for a moment, then Lucy spoke. "Charlie, what's going on?"

"What do you think is going on?" The bounder had the nerve to laugh.

The rush of tears streaming down Lucy's face broke my heart. The poor thing didn't say another word. She took the key from the lock, closed the bedroom door, and locked it from the outside.

"Come on, Lucy, don't be a bloody cow," Charles demanded.

She walked, head held high, down to the kitchen, picked up a long wooden spoon, wrapped it in a cloth, then stuck it in the firebox. With a torch in one hand, and a pile of rags in the other, she climbed the stairs again. She stuffed the rags under the door and lit them. She then went into every room lighting blankets and curtains on fire.

I screamed as loud as I could from my crackling walls to my shattering windows, but no one came to save me. Lucy sat in the parlour, drinking whiskey and lighting candles. Then, she walked around my main floor, lighting every room on fire. When she was finished, she lay down on her brocade sofa, took another gulp of whiskey, poured the rest over her body, and closed her eyes.

I was ash by the time dear Perry arrived. When his mother hadn't shown up at the college, he sensed something was wrong and came racing home. He now stood at the edge of the sidewalk, gazing at my portrait in his hands. It was to have been an early birthday gift for his beloved mother. Waves of his grief drifted through the air until they reached my remains. I grabbed hold of them, rode them back to the portrait, and settled myself in for a journey to another time and place.

I stand on the sidewalk gazing at the spectre that is Camellia Manor, a late Victorian home painted pink with white and brown trim. I breathe in the strong, sweet scent of the lilacs growing along the pathway. A few feet away, at the side of the house, the elm tree flutters its leaves, dancing in the gentle breeze. The red birdhouse affixed to its trunk is filled with birds I cannot name. Their happy music lightens my soul.

I recall the last thing Sabrina said when she sold me the painting. *A time will come when the doors and windows of the manor are slammed shut forever.*

I inch my way along the path and slowly climb the wooden steps to the front door. I glance around at the red camellias sitting in pots on the porch and hanging from the eaves in earthen baskets. It will be the last time I see them.

The house calls me to enter.

I give one last thought to my son. Simon will be furious that I've left him behind, that I've left him an orphan. He wouldn't have understood even if I'd explained it all to him. All that this house meant to me. All this house has done to me. All this house has played in his own life.

I left him ignorant of my crimes. *A good mother, a kind mother, the best mother,* I hope he'll say when I disappear.

I turn the china door handle and step inside. The familiar aroma of freshly baked cinnamon buns greets me. My heart thumps as I realize what this means. Jack has prepared our anniversary treat. I run to the kitchen. He isn't there but the tray is filled with the evidence of his love. I pick it up and skip up the stairs to the bedroom.

The front door slams shut behind me.

After Louise's disappearance, Simon sold me back to the Queen Moonfall Curio Shop. Sabrina has once again hung me on the back wall. My rose-quartz frame and ruby-red camellias on the brown moonstone porch are an invitation, a calling, an urging, a temptation for potential buyers to turn the pearl handle of the opal-white door and enter. It's been over a year since I trapped Louise within my walls. I long for someone new to occupy my days. But I'm hidden in a small corner among the lobster traps and tangled ropes. Hardly anyone comes my way. I'm completely ignored.

The doorbell jingles. Anxiety rises in me as I wait to see if I'm chosen. A pretty brunette strolls around the shop, flicking her hair and lifting up knickknack after knickknack. I whisper "Over here" several times. Eventually, she picks her way through the mess of tools in front of me and peers closely. She smiles. My walls vibrate with excitement. Will she be the one?

"Oh, my, what a lovely painting?" She turns to the man who accompanies her. "I must have it, darling."

My interior pulses with overwhelming gratitude. My windows sparkle and gleam.

The next adventure has begun. And it will be this woman's turn to tell the story.

ACKNOWLEDGEMENTS

Thank you to the staff, instructors, and fellow writers at the Alexandra Writers' Centre Society, who have taught me, encouraged me, and supported me along the way. A special thank you to my friends, Louise and Laura-Jeanne, who have critiqued many versions of my story. Thank you Lexie for this opportunity to be published by Radical Bookshop and Press. Also, thank you to my editor, Charlotte Hayes-Clemens, who offered the best suggestions and advice. It was a pleasure to work with you, Charlotte. A big shout out to my Write Now crew who keep writing their own wonderful stories. Remember every day—write a word, a sentence, a paragraph, or a page, and soon the world will have the pleasure of reading your published stories.

ABOUT THE AUTHOR

Cindy Webb Morris was born in a mansion during a hurricane and raised in a hunting camp in the backwoods of New Brunswick, Canada. She enjoys writing fiction in a variety of genres and is currently working on first drafts of two novels, a screenplay, and several short stories. Cindy has published a couple of short stories in Canada and the UK, a flash fiction piece, an essay, a newspaper article, and a couple of poems. She uses her Management Certificate in Workplace Communication from the University of Calgary in her volunteer work with the Alexandra Writers' Centre Society, where she is a board member, volunteer coordinator, one-woman welcome committee, and leader of the writing group, Write Now. Cindy loves being involved in supporting writers and can often be heard sharing her views on the importance of being part of a community of like-minded people.

www.ingramcontent.com/pod-product-compliance
Lightning Source LLC
Chambersburg PA
CBHW030013010826
48973CB00009B/2791

9 781990 201189